FOOTBA
LEGENDS

LIONEL MESSI

E.L. NORRY

FOOTBALL LEGENDS

LIONEL MESSI

SCHOLASTIC

Scholastic Australia
PO Box 579 Gosford NSW 2250
ABN 11 000 614 577
www.scholastic.com.au

Part of the Scholastic Group
Sydney • Auckland • New York • Toronto • London • Mexico City
New Delhi • Hong Kong • Buenos Aires • Puerto Rico

First published in the UK by Scholastic Ltd in 2021.
This edition published by Scholastic Australia in 2024.

While this book is based on real characters and actual historical events, some situations and people are fictional, created by the author.

UNAUTHORIZED: this book is not sponsored, approved or endorsed by any person who appears in this book.

ISBN 978-1-76152-740-1

Printed in China by Hang Tai Printing Company Limited.

MIX
Paper | Supporting responsible forestry
FSC® C023121
FSC www.fsc.org

10 9 8 7 6 5 4 3 2 24 25 26 27 28 / 2

Contents

FOOTBALL LEGENDS

At break time in the playground there is trouble. An argument happening in one corner of the playing field. An older, taller boy and a younger one are having the same argument they often do, about football, and who they think the best ever player is.

"Ronaldo is the best player in the world!" the bigger boy says. He shoves the younger boy, who stumbles and falls onto the grass.

He jumps back up and yells, "No, he isn't. Messi is!"

"Ronaldo!" shouts the older boy.

"Messi is better."

"Tell me why then!"

"Have you seen Messi assist?"

"So? Ronaldo is strong."

"Strength isn't everything! Messi has natural talent. He does something once and then can do it right away. He's a team player and makes everyone around him play better."

"So what? Messi hasn't even won any international titles! And he is tiny, too small. Ronaldo is big and strong and tall! His headers are the best!"

1

MESSI – THE GREATEST FOOTBALLER EVER?

Each generation has had a 'greatest football player' that most fans could agree on.

The Brazilian legend, Pelé, played at four World Cups and was part of three winning Brazil teams in 1958, 1962 and 1970. He was strong in all areas, blessed with incredible vision, technical skill and creativity. He could shoot, he was fast, he could hold the ball. On top of this, he was an admired and proud ambassador of the game, even after his playing career was over. In the 1970s there were many English schoolboys who were proud to wear a Brazilian football shirt with his name on the back.

In the 1980s, Diego Maradona led Argentina to World Cup glory, winning many of their important games almost single-handedly. This was another footballing genius, a player who was strong in every part of the game. He was incredibly quick and nimble and could dribble through the smallest of gaps (as his famous World Cup goal against England showed). Although relatively short, he seemed to have springs in his boots, which allowed him to score plenty of headers. He scored amazing goals with either foot. Although some of his behaviour in his personal life later on led to public criticism, his footballing talent could not be denied.

Now, at the start of the twenty-first century, football fans have found themselves with a more difficult question to answer. We have been blessed with two geniuses playing at the same time! And often playing against each other in the same game.

Cristiano Ronaldo, the Portuguese superstar with model looks, has played brilliantly for three of the greatest European clubs in football: Manchester United, Real Madrid and Juventus. He has five Champions League winner's medals and has received five Ballon d'Or awards. He is an incredible athlete and scores spectacular goals with both feet. He is also able to outjump defenders with ease to score with his head. His free kicks are terrifyingly powerful and accurate. Given that sports technology and training methods have improved so much over the years, it could be argued that this would make him a stronger player than the legends that went before him, including Maradona and Pelé. However, there is still one player to consider …

Lionel Messi was born in Argentina, but he moved to Spain to play for Barcelona when he was just thirteen, and he has played for the same team ever since. He has won La Liga (the Spanish league) ten times, the Champions League four times, and the Ballon d'Or six times. He is smaller than the average player, and is dwarfed by his tall, muscular rival, Ronaldo. Although he can also score great goals with both feet, if they went up to compete for a header, Ronaldo would probably win every time. But, like his hero Maradona, who was also a short player, Messi's height does give him an advantage over his rival: a low centre of gravity. This is vital to his style of play, as it means he has superb balance. This allows his quick feet to dribble the ball at high speed in and out of the smallest spaces. If a player can be said to have a superpower, Messi's is dribbling.

But Who is the Best Player – Ronaldo or Messi?

Because they are recognised as two of the greatest players of all time, and because they faced each other many times while Ronaldo was playing for the mighty Real Madrid, the discussions and debates about who is the better footballer have been inevitable and ongoing.

The answer depends on who you ask. Few Real Madrid fans are likely to give their vote to Messi. Zinedine Zidane, the legendary French footballer, has said that he rates Ronaldo higher than Messi. But Ronaldo did help Zidane win three Champions League titles in a row as Real Madrid manager.

Ronaldo has physical advantages in terms of height and strength, but many experts believe that Messi has the edge. They see him as a better team player, able to involve his teammates and improve their performances. They also refer to Messi's 'magic', his greater natural talent. He can unlock defences with a variety of skills, from his dribbling to his laser-guided passes.

Regardless of the answer, it is clear both players regard each other with the utmost respect. Ronaldo left Madrid in 2018 to go and play for Italian giants Juventus, and Messi has said that he misses playing against him. In an interview he said, "It was nice playing against Cristiano even if it was difficult. I enjoyed winning cups when he was at Madrid. It would be nice if he were still there … I have a lot of respect for Juventus; I think they are a very strong team, with very good players – and with the arrival of Cristiano, even more so."

And Ronaldo has said about Messi: "For me rivals don't exist … rivals in a war, in football, no, it's just a game. I think the numbers, they say everything. I'd like him to come to Italy one day. I hope he accepts the challenge like me, but if he's happy there then I respect that. He's a fantastic player and a good guy, but I don't miss anything here."

For now, perhaps we can give the last word on this debate to Jürgen Klopp, Liverpool's manager, who has managed many great players but has no personal history with either: "I have one selfie on my smartphone. That's with Messi. Cristiano was in the room as well …

2

MOVING ON UP

Lionel Messi (Luis Lionel Andrés 'Leo' Messi) was born 24 June 1987 in Rosario, Argentina, South America.

Lionel's family weren't poor but they weren't rich either. They were what is known as 'middle-class'. Lionel's dad, Jorge, worked in a steel factory and his mother, Celia, had different jobs, including one as a part-time cleaner. Lionel has two older brothers, Rodrigo and Matias, and a younger sister called Maria.

Some people call Messi by the nickname La Pulga, which means 'The Flea' in Spanish – because he is small and quick and gets into everywhere!

These days he plays left-footed as number 10 in the forward position for Barcelona and the Argentina national team. Many believe Lionel Messi is one of the greatest footballers of all time! His modesty and manners are well known, and he doesn't play-act on the pitch, dive or argue with referees, unlike more dramatic players such as Cristiano Ronaldo. Although Lionel is a little quiet, he has no problem expressing himself on the pitch, where it really counts.

Lionel's short stature (5 feet, 7 inches), combined with his speed and persistent attacking style, has, over the years, drawn comparisons to the other world-famous football player from Argentina: Diego Maradona. Although the two players have different personalities and came from different backgrounds, people still like to talk about their similarities.

Lionel's dedication to football over the past twenty years proves that there is nothing that can't be achieved if you are willing to work hard.

Aged thirteen, Lionel moved to Barcelona, Spain, from his home in Rosario, Argentina. Eventually, FC Barcelona agreed to sign him, and he joined their footballing academy. The team paid for his medical treatment and he was able to get the growth hormones he needed.

Spanish football league system

La Liga (which has twenty teams) is the highest level, followed by Segunda División A and then Segunda División B.

The football season is August to May. Each FC club plays every other club twice: once at home and once away, for thirty-eight match days. If the team win they get three points, if they draw it's one point and a loss earns no points. The team that has the most points at the end of the season is the overall winner.

Whichever three teams are placed lowest in La Liga are relegated to the Segunda División. The top two teams from the Segunda División are promoted to La Liga. And, after a series of playoffs, involving the third-, fourth-, fifth- and sixth-placed clubs, another club will be promoted.

Lionel Messi has always remained loyal to the same team despite receiving offers to join other teams. Playing for Barcelona he has earned the reputation as one of the greatest players in history. He has helped his club win more than two dozen league titles and tournaments. In 2012, he set a record for scoring the most goals in a calendar year, and in 2019, he was named Europe's Ballon d'Or winner for the sixth time. As Luka Modrić handed it over he said to Lionel, "You deserve it."

His contract with FC Barcelona is due to end in 2021, so who knows what might be next for the footballer with plenty of energy left? He has said how special his home in Rosario is and the first club he played for, Newell's Old Boys. Perhaps that might be next for him?

Let's find out how a smaller than average boy grew up to become one of the best footballers in the world …

Early Days

It seems that football was always destined to be a huge part of Lionel's life, from when he was really young.

The Messi family were close and grandparents and two cousins, Emanuel and Maximiliano, lived nearby. Lionel's mum, Celia, remembers that the cousins (who also went on to be professional footballers) used to play football when they visited their grandmother for Sunday lunch.

Lionel says, "As a child, I always had a ball nearby. I liked every sport, but football was the one I liked the most. At home, everybody was crazy about football: my brothers, my cousins, everyone. We all played football – it was the most important thing in our lives … My first memories are from when I was very little, maybe three or four years old, playing in my neighbourhood at home. I can picture myself with the ball at my feet from a very young age."

Famously, he received his first football as a birthday present when he was just four years old. He liked it so much that he sometimes slept with it!

Sad News

Sadly, when Lionel was only eleven, his grandmother died. She'd been a huge supporter and was a big influence on him and everyone missed her. Sometimes, even now, when he scores a goal, he reaches his arms up to the sky, as if dedicating his success to her.

STARTING OUT

Lionel's two older brothers, Rodrigo and Matias, played football for the local team, which was called Grandoli FC. Rodrigo played centre forward and Matias was a defender. Grandoli's pitch wasn't fancy – there was barely any grass and it had an uneven surface of rocks and stones – but it was still somewhere to play.

Lionel's grandma used to take the boys to their training twice a week and Lionel would go along to watch them play. He was very close to his grandma, and she was one of the first to notice his talent. This led to one of Lionel first opportunities to play and show the adults how talented he already was, what natural ability he had.

Lionel started playing with Grandoli FC when he was only four.

"When I started, we were playing in a seven-a-side league, against other little teams from the southern neighbourhoods of Rosario. I only got the chance to play as young as I did because of my grandmother. Grandoli didn't have a team for boys as young as me but, one Sunday, an older boy didn't turn up for his game and my grandmother pushed me forward to play. The coach wasn't keen at first, but he let me play in the end."

During the game, it took a little while for Lionel to demonstrate his skills, but after a while he dribbled the ball down the pitch. Even though the coach, Salvador Aparicio, wasn't impressed at first, Lionel soon proved that he had talent.

A year later, his dad, Jorge, became the team's coach. With Lionel on their side, the team did well. They won all their games: friendlies, tournaments and the championship! Lionel became well known in the neighbourhood.

Newell's Old Boys

The next big step towards Lionel becoming the professional footballer he is today came when he was aged eight. He was recruited to join Newell's Old Boys, a Rosario-based club. Newell's was a football club that meant a lot to the Messi family. Lionel's dad, Jorge, had played for them when he was a teenager and his brothers both joined too.

"After a year and a half at Grandoli, I started training with Newell's too; also seven-a-side, but we played in a more competitive league. Newell's was a much bigger club and my last year there gave me my first experience of playing eleven-a-side on a full-sized pitch."

Lionel was part of the team called La Maquina del '87, named because all the players were born in the same year. This made the playing fair and equal. The team played together for six years. As you can imagine, they got to know each other very well. The 'Machine of '87' became very successful and won matches and tournaments all over Argentina. Lionel was their top scorer.

Growing Pains

During Lionel years playing for Newell's, his parents decided to take him to see a doctor. Aged around nine, Messi had stopped growing any bigger – he was ten centimeters smaller than most other boys his age. Something definitely wasn't right.

"I had always been smaller than other boys of my age, but it didn't really worry me when it came to football. Perhaps at the start of a game I could tell that other boys were looking at me and that made me feel uncomfortable but, once we kicked off, they saw how I played and there'd be no problems after that! So I never thought of it as something to worry about."

Lionel had many tests. Eventually, he was diagnosed by a specialist (an endocrinologist) as suffering from a hormone deficiency. This was restricting his growth. The condition was treatable, so Jorge and Celia decided to pay for their son to receive treatment, which involved Lionel injecting a growth hormone into his legs every night. Nothing was going to stand in his way of playing football!

Messi's medication cost several hundred pounds per month and although at first, because his family had health insurance, this wasn't a problem, paying for the treatment soon became more complicated. After a while, affording the treatment proved impossible for Lionel's parents – they had three other children to think about.

Newell's football club stepped in to help financially for a while, but unfortunately, this didn't work out either. When another football club in Buenos Aires thought they might sign Lionel there was another spark of hope, but the deal never happened.

What could be done? Carrying on with Lionel's treatment was a good idea. If he was going to continue playing football he'd need to reach his full size, and live up to his early potential … Jorge and Celia needed to make some decisions about what was best for their whole family.

4
MORE THAN A CLUB

General Franco ruled Spain from 1939 until he died in 1975. The way he ruled meant that he was a dictator. He was known for the way he bullied the Catalan people (Catalonia is the area of Spain where Barcelona is – Catalans are fiercely proud of their region and many people there regard themselves as separate to the rest of Spain). Franco didn't keep it a secret that he preferred Real Madrid as a football team. This explains the long history of competition between the two teams. The FC Barcelona (nickname Barca) official motto is "More than just a club" – this shows how the club became a symbol of unity for the Catalans, who were used to being the underdog.

So, how did a footballer from Argentina end up playing for one of the top Spanish football clubs?

A sports agent named Josep Maria Minguella had heard about Lionel's skills playing for Newell's. He sent a videotape of Lionel playing to a friend of his, Carles Rexach, who was one of the football scouts for FC Barcelona.

Sports agent: someone who looks after a footballer's interests. They help deal with their finances and contracts, as well as advise. For this, they get a portion of the player's earnings.

Football scout: these go to local matches and watch players who might have potential to play for a larger club.

Although Rexach could see Lionel's talents, at first he was concerned that he was too young and too small. However, he still invited Lionel out to Barcelona for a two-week trial.

Lionel and his dad, Jorge, arrived in Barcelona in September 2000.

But Barcelona weren't making any commitments – yes, they could see he was talented, but he was young and had hormone treatment that needed paying for. Also, they didn't often work with players who lived outside Spain. The majority of their players came from Spain, usually from Barcelona's surrounding areas.

Barcelona had their own youth football training academy called La Masia: an eighteenth-century farmhouse just across the street from the stadium, set up in the 1970s. Scouts searched everywhere for boys aged between six to eleven who might become the next big talent, and if the boys were picked then they received free education and football training.

Contract on a Paper Napkin

Other clubs had also shown an interest in Lionel. Minguella and another sports agent took Rexach out to dinner and told him that he had to make a decision on whether or not he was going to sign Lionel, and soon. Everyone was getting sick of waiting around.

December 2000, it finally happened. Rexach kept his promise. Since no one had any paper at the time, he wrote on a paper napkin, "I, Charly Rexach, in my capacity as technical secretary for FC Barcelona, and despite the existence of some opinions against it, commit to signing Lionel Messi as long as the conditions agreed are met."

FC Barcelona offered to pay Lionel's medical bills, and with this brilliant opportunity now secure, the Messi family made the bold decision to move across the Atlantic and set up a new home in Spain.

Lionel says, "When I arrived in Barcelona, my dream was to play in the first team, but I never could've imagined what would happen next! We visited the city like tourists – Barca's stadium is beautiful, and I still remember the emotion I felt the first time I stepped foot onto the Camp Nou."

Camp Nou is Barca's home stadium. Lionel's dream had come true aged thirteen. He and his family lived in an apartment on Gran Via de Carles III, near the stadium, so he didn't sleep at La Maisa, although others did. He went to Leon XIII school where other La Maisa boys also studied, and trained with them at the footballing academy.

Lionel was often homesick in his new country, even though he progressed swiftly through the junior system ranks.

5

FOOTBALL LEGENDS

OVERCOMING CHALLENGES

Even though Barcelona had decided that they wanted Messi and he was very keen to start playing, there were issues which stopped him playing straight away. His old team, Newell's Old Boys, and the AFA (Argentine Football Association) wouldn't sign the paperwork allowing him to transfer to FC Barcelona. So, although he was part of the team, he could only play in friendly matches and wasn't allowed to play in any national or international matches! Not only that but Messi also suffered a few injuries in April and May 2001 meaning that he couldn't play at all for weeks. Can you imagine how disappointing that must have been?

Messi said, "I was happy to be living in Barcelona and experiencing all those new things. On the other hand, it was hard to be so far away from people. I had to start again: new teammates, new friends. I also couldn't play at first because of injury and because there were problems with the paperwork. That start was hard."

In 2001, for the summer, the whole family headed back home to Rosario. Jorge asked Lionel if he wanted to stay in Rosario or go back to Barcelona – Lionel wanted to go back; he wanted to play for Barcelona. But his brothers missed their friends and Maria wasn't enjoying school in Barcelona, so although it was a difficult decision, Celia decided it'd be better for them to stay in Rosario. Jorge and Lionel returned to Barcelona on their own.

Jaume Marcet, a Barca TV journalist, recalls Messi's exasperating beginnings. "I would see him at the games not even sat on the bench but in street clothes because he was not allowed to play … he had come all this way to play and he was not able to."

But FIFA got involved, and eventually Newell's Old Boys gave their permission. Messi could start showing off his magic!

PART OF THE TEAM

In Barcelona, Messi struggled to make friends and feel part of the team because he was extremely shy.

About the others at La Maisa he says, "They also knew what it was like to be far from their families and friends, so we had a lot in common. I had a hard time during the first two seasons."

"We thought he was mute," Cesc Fàbregas remembered later. "Until he picked up the ball, and then any doubts were gone," said Gerard Piqué.

Messi came out of his shell a bit more during the 2002 Maestrelli tournament in Italy – his first with Barcelona.

The team had four captains: Fàbregas, Piqué, Marc Valiente and Víctor Vázquez, and as a sort of welcome, they liked to play jokes on squad members who were new.

"When we arrived at the hotel, Messi had brought his PlayStation with him and went to his room with Cesc, who he was sharing with," Vázquez recalls, the team's centre forward. "Piqué decided to go and take everything out of his room, as if it had been robbed. We went down for dinner and Gerard arrived late, as they had ransacked it. They took out the bed, his PlayStation, kitbag – literally everything. After we had eaten, everyone went back up to their rooms and Cesc and a couple of other players recorded Messi going into his room. He stood stock-still. His face was a picture! He didn't know what to say because he was quite a shy lad, and so he just put his hands on his head. Then we told him it was something that we did to every new player. He really opened up after that."

Lionel's teammates enjoyed messing around. They weren't trying to be mean, they all liked having a laugh and breaking up their intensive training with some light relief. Thankfully, Messi found it funny, eventually! And by the end of the trip, Messi was playing the jokes.

"After that, he was totally different," Julio De Dios said. "He was making jokes, and I think he got Piqué back with some prank. 'Now Messi's arrived!' we'd say, patting him on the back. From that moment he became one of us. We were a cohort of brothers."

At La Maisa, after evening training session, players had dinner at 8 pm before having free time. They played PlayStation tournaments which took about a week to complete – everyone huddled around the computer screen. "Fàbregas was pretty good and so was Piqué,' recalls De Dios. "But Messi was a disaster! As time went on, he did get better, but he was terrible at the beginning. On the PlayStation he was awful, but on the pitch he was the best."

The other good news during this time was that Messi finished his hormone treatments. Although still on the smaller side, he'd reached his full height of 5 feet nearly 7 inches.

STAR POTENTIAL

By now, Messi was playing for the B team, playing on the wing but frequently moving into a more central position. Pere Gratacós looked after the B team in 2003 and said Messi was an extraordinary player who did things with ease.

In November, Frank Rijkaard, the coach of FC Barcelona, had a problem – some of his top players on the A team were injured and he needed players for a friendly against Porto. Gratacós recommended Messi. So Rijkaard promoted some players from Barcelona B squad to the first team, including Messi.

Messi's debut was on 16 November, but he failed

to score. The match was only a one-off though, and afterwards Messi was back playing for the B team. He trained once a week with the A team, got to know many of the players, who were really impressed with his talent, and after a year was invited to join them for good.

Messi didn't have to wait long to make an amazing impression: his debut aged seventeen, in October 2004, against Espanyol. He was Barcelona's second-youngest player ever to play for their A team.

Seven months later on 1 May 2005, Messi became the youngest ever goalscorer when Ronaldinho flicked the ball over the defence and with a deft chip, Messi scored.

FIFA Under-20 World Cup

When the AFA asked him if he wanted to join Argentina's Under-20s national team, he agreed. He said he would be proud to represent his country. In 2005, the Under-20s squad was one out of twenty-four teams who qualified for the FIFA World Cup in Holland. The team finished second in their group and advanced to the knockout stages. Messi performed brilliantly and their success was largely to do with him: he scored more goals than anyone else – six – during the tournament. His coaches and teammates were very happy with his performance. He also led Argentina to the World Cup U-20 title, scoring from two penalties to propel the team ahead of Nigeria.

He said, "one day when I was sixteen, I was called up to play in two friendlies with the U-20 team against Paraguay and Uruguay – the beginning of my journey. We won the U-20 World Cup in Netherlands, one of the biggest achievements in my career."

Barca's Baby Dream Team

Some football fans believe the three players who came out of La Maisa – Lionel Messi, Cesc Fàbregas and Gerard Piqué – were the greatest youth team Barcelona has ever had. They became known as the Baby Dream Team, (also known as Generation '87 or Class of 2002). They won La Liga and the Catalan and Spanish championships. Messi was the top scorer as a second striker with thirty goals in thirty-seven games. Piqué marshalled the defence and Fàbregas was a midfielder.

La Maisa had many different divisions and teams, and over eighteen months Messi played for various teams, both A and B. His coaches said he never complained because he just loved playing football and always gave his best.

Albert Benaiges was the youth coach and has memories of Messi aged fifteen, notably his ability and positive attitude. The academy wasn't only focused on talent but on bringing up the boys to have good old-fashioned values and manners too.

"He did something that says so much about him because a lot of young kids don't like doing it. In one year he played with the Barca C youth team, then Barca B and then with Barca A. But then he went back and played for Barca C again afterwards. You could say to him, 'Look here's the ball, let's play a match,' and he would get on with it. He just loved playing. He didn't mind what level. Some kids when they play for the A team and then you ask them to play for the B team they pull a face, but with him he always gave everything."

In the summer of 2003, Fàbregas moved on

to play for Arsenal, and Piqué went to play for Manchester United (he would come back to Barcelona in 2008).

The Game of the Mask

At the end of the 2003 season, playing a league title Copa Catalunya deciding match, Messi collided with an opponent and fractured his cheekbone. No one thought he'd be able to play in the final a few days later. After seeking medical advice, he was told he could play, but *only* if he wore the protective face-covering mask. But, only a few minutes in, he took the plastic mask off, saying he couldn't play with it on because it made him sweat and he couldn't see properly. He begged to play a while longer and then managed to score twice!

MAGICAL MOMENTS

In such a long and illustrious career it's difficult to pick out all the highlights but these matches regularly feature in Lionel Messi's interviews and commentators' favourite matches. Let's remember what they felt like!

Messi crowns his World Cup debut with a goal

(Argentina 6–0 Serbia and Montenegro, World Cup, group stage, 16 June 16 2006)

This game marked Messi's first appearance at the World Cup, at the age of eighteen. Although he was already regarded as a remarkable talent and had featured in many friendly matches for Argentina, he was still relatively inexperienced at senior level. He remained on the bench as a substitute for the whole of Argentina's first group game against Ivory Coast, which Argentina won 2–1 after a very competitive match.

He found himself on the bench again for the second game against Serbia and Montenegro, and although Messi was incredibly excited about getting out onto the pitch to play his first World Cup game, he had to be patient. Finally, the manager summoned his young star to join the action in the seventy-fourth minute. By the time his big moment arrived, Argentina already had a comfortable 3–0 lead. In some ways, this was the perfect moment to make his entrance. The game was almost certainly won at this point, and Messi would be free to express himself without the pressure of needing to score.

It took him only four minutes to show the world his incredible footballing skills. Having collected a low pass on the left, he sprinted at top speed down the wing. He angled his run into the eighteen-yard box, before sliding a pinpoint pass behind the defence, into the path of Hernán Crespo, who scored the easiest of goals.

A couple of minutes before the end of the game, Lionel would get the chance to experience the moment he had dreamed of – scoring his first World Cup goal. After a series of quick, clever passes outside the opposition's box, Carlos Tevez played a diagonal pass out to the right. Messi accelerated onto the through-ball with lightning pace, outran his defender and slipped the ball under the flailing feet of the keeper. This momentous goal came as no surprise to the English match commentator, who exclaimed, "It's Messi – he just had to score!" Messi later described the feeling in one word: "Beautiful!"

The new Maradona is born!

(Barcelona 5–2 Getafe, Copa del Rey, semi-final, 18 April 2007)

"I've always measured my goals by the importance of them, not for the beauty."

Some goals, like some football games, are remembered for their importance. The goal that wins the Champion's League Final. The goal that decides the result of El Clásico (a game between rivals FC Barcelona and Real Madrid). However, there are other goals which are like a rare treasure, a wondrous work of art. These are remembered for their pure perfection. Their beauty is unforgettable.

In the 1986 World Cup, during a quarter-final match between England and Argentina, Diego Maradona, one of the greatest players of all time, treated the footballing world to one of these beautiful gems. Earlier in the game, he had created controversy with a far-from-beautiful goal which was scored (illegally) with a high, sly knock from his left hand. The goal stood, and the England fans were furious. Later in the same game, he atoned for his earlier sin. Collecting the ball in his own half, he danced and span, the ball magnetised to his feet, skipping away from his markers. Off he sped into the England half, darting one way, then another. No one could touch him – he was flowing. Finally, he rounded the keeper and as the last defender made a desperate lunge from behind, Diego slotted an angled shot into the open net. *Goooaaaal!*

Fast forward nearly twenty-one years, and

another small Argentinian player finds himself collecting the ball on the right wing in his own half. He too is under pressure from opposition players immediately. But this is another special player, with superhuman awareness and instincts. He escapes his opponents with a few delicate flicks, and he is away. With incredible speed and balance, he sprints into the opposition half, following almost exactly the same path furrowed by his hero. Two Getafe players are in hot pursuit, and two more are waiting ahead, determined to halt his progress. Defenders lunge at him from all angles, but his skittering feet are much too quick – he is gone before they arrive. He doesn't even need to think about the ball now; it is completely under his spell. He waits for the exact millisecond that the keeper begins to dive at his feet, then drags the ball to his right and slots an angled shot into the net. *Goooaaal!*

Like Maradona's goal, this one would live in the memories of football fans long after the details and significance of the game itself were forgotten. The game ended with a comfortable 5–2 win for Barcelona, so Messi's goal did not decide the result. Nor was the game key to the team's success that season. But apart from being beautiful, the goal was important in another way. It announced the arrival of a new footballing genius.

Messi's international honour

(Argentina 1–0 Nigeria, Beijing Olympic Games, 23 August 2008)

In Lionel's own words, "the Olympics are very important, not only for the opportunity to win a medal for your country, but also the experience of being able to take part in an amazing global event and live in the Olympic village with athletes from so many different sports.

It was incredible – a complete tournament for us. Yes, we won the semi-final 3–0 against Brazil – a great team who were also playing well – but we also overcame the Netherlands and Nigeria. Both were very hard games and we had to be at our best to win. We were very confident that we could claim the gold medal. Look at the team we had and the unity among the players. We thought from the start that we could win in Beijing and we were able to do it."

Messi, the 'false nine', provides a tactical victory in El Clásico

(Real Madrid 2–6 Barcelona, La Liga, 2 May 2009)

Lionel Messi has been involved in many epic battles with Barcelona's arch-rivals, Real Madrid, over the years. By Messi's own admission, El Clásico was always a big challenge, and the result was always hard to predict: "Those big matches can go either way, and I've been in games where we've conceded four goals to Real."

On this occasion, Barcelona would come away as convincing winners. One of the main reasons for their impressive victory was the tactical skill and bravery of their legendary coach, Pep Guardiola. After studying recordings of Madrid's recent matches very carefully, he came up with a brilliant idea. He summoned Messi to his office the day before the game, and he explained that he wanted his star player to play in an unusual position – the 'false nine'.

Messi has been asked to play in various positions

as his footballing career developed. For some time now, Messi has usually been positioned on the right side of an attacking front three. However, in his earliest days in Argentina he played behind the playmaker in midfield. Then, when he first arrived at Barcelona, he played at the front of the midfield diamond formation. For this game, he would learn about a new position he had never been asked to play in.

But what is a false nine?

Basically, this is a striker who drops deep, drifting back into midfield rather than staying around the penalty box as a normal centre forward would (note: in the old days, the centre forward wore the number nine shirt). A few other teams had experimented with this tactic in the past, the first being the Austrian national team of the 1930s. The famous Italian player Francesco Totti had played the same role for Roma in 2006–7. The intention was to confuse and unsettle the opposition's central defenders, who were unsure where they should be positioning themselves from moment to moment.

On this night at the Bernabéu, Messi played the false-nine role to perfection. Aside from creating space for him to score two goals, it allowed him to drop deep and play defence-splitting passes, and it opened up all sorts of opportunities for his quick, wide players. This was the first time in the history of El Clásico that the away team had scored six goals. It also paved the way for Barcelona's nineteenth La Liga title.

He said, "It was a fantastic performance from the whole team. I'm not sure whether it was the best, but it's certainly a match that we will always remember and cherish."

Messi scores in his first Champion's League Final victory

(Barcelona 2–0 Manchester United, Champions League final, 27 May 2009)

This match was one of many famous encounters with Messi's greatest rival. Cristiano Ronaldo is the only current player to have won more Champion League titles than Messi, and to have scored more goals in the competition. However, on this occasion, Lionel eventually came out on top.

Messi had won the title with Barcelona previously in 2006, but he suffered a torn hamstring against Chelsea in the last sixteen round. He did not manage to return to full fitness in time for the final against Arsenal. He was very upset that he was not in Paris to celebrate his team's victory.

His big chance to make up for this disappointment arrived in May 2009. However, it would not be an easy task. Their opponents, Manchester United, were the current champions of Europe. Apart from Ronaldo, the team also included the powerful forward Wayne Rooney, and one of the strongest defences in the competition.

United started the game well, putting Barcelona under pressure early on. However, in the tenth minute of the game, Barcelona's first serious attack resulted in a fantastic individual goal from their speedy and skilful centre forward, Samuel Eto'o.

It was a very competitive match, and Ronaldo fought hard, doing his best to threaten Barcelona's goal. But despite going close a few times, he was struggling to find the target. Equally, Messi and Barcelona had several chances, but they could not find the decisive second goal. At one point during the second half, Messi burst into the opponents' box. He was about to receive a pass, but at the crucial moment went sprawling to the ground. He raised his arms in the air in protest, insisting he had been dragged back by a defender. But the referee waved to play on.

With twenty minutes of the game left, Barcelona's gifted playmaker, Xavi, found himself approaching the right-hand corner of the eighteen-yard box. For once, this stubborn United defence had left him with plenty of space and time to decide his next move. With a quick look up, he spotted his teammate Lionel drifting in towards the far corner of the six-yard box. This was their chance! Xavi curled the ball high into the air. Messi ghosted in behind the giant United defender, Rio Ferdinand, leapt into the air, and headed the ball up and over the United keeper into the far corner of the net. *Goal!* 2–0 to Barcelona!

Messi later said, "It was hard to imagine that I was going to score with my head with Ferdinand standing near me, but I didn't really have a marker – the ball came into the centre and I was there to meet it … It's still one of my favourite goals."

Messi's beautiful goal wins an ugly war

(Barcelona 2–0 Real Madrid, Champions League semi-final, 27 April 2011)

This was always going to be a hard-fought and passionate game. The two giants of Spanish football, Real Madrid and Barcelona, were to lock horns yet again. But this time, there was an added ingredient: securing a place in the final of the biggest club competition in the world, the Champions League. The El Clásico derby happens twice a year in La Liga, and those games are always fearsome battles. This was only the second time these teams had crossed paths in the Champions League, and each side was one step away from the final destination and the ultimate footballing prize. A war was inevitable.

Straight from the whistle, the game set off at a very fast pace. It wasn't long before there were vicious tackles flying in all over the pitch. Even when the aggressive kicks and shoves missed their target, players would throw themselves to the ground, as if they had been shot by a gun, trying to win a free kick from the referee. There were forty-five fouls committed (one foul every two minutes on average!). There were five yellow cards and two reds. One of those red cards was issued to Barcelona's substitute goalkeeper, José Manuel Pinto, at the end of half-time, while he was still on the bench! He had got himself into a heated argument with some of the Madrid team at the side of the pitch.

The beautiful game was turning ugly, and it

was becoming an impossible match for the referee to control. It certainly didn't suit Messi's old rival, Ronaldo, who appeared out of sorts and struggled to find his form. Players had very little time on the ball – anyone who held on to it too long would soon find themselves battered to the ground.

The tide suddenly turned in Barcelona's favour in the sixty-first minute. Madrid's Pepe was sent off for a horrible tackle that left Barcelona's Dani Alves writhing on the floor, clutching his shin in agony. With Madrid reduced to ten men, there was now just a little more space for Barcelona and their Argentinian magician to play in.

They had to wait until the seventy-sixth minute to grab the opening goal. Five minutes after coming onto the pitch, the substitute winger Ibrahim Afellay received the ball on the right wing, just outside the eighteen-yard box. A quick burst of pace took him past the defender, and from the by-line he whipped a low ball across the face of the goal. Messi accelerated into the box, ghosting in between three defenders to pop the ball into the net at the near post. *Goal!*

Barcelona had that valuable away goal, which

would virtually count as two goals for the second leg. But Barcelona were not finished yet. A few minutes before the final whistle, Messi collected the ball deep in Madrid's half, just beyond the centre circle. Already running at pace, he gained momentum, accelerating past one, two, three, four Madrid players. As he approached the six-yard box from the right, with the last defender hurtling desperately towards him, he placed the ball to the left of the flailing keeper with his (weaker) right foot. The ball nestled beautifully into the bottom corner of the net. Messi had ensured victory for Barcelona, winning an ugly game with one of his most beautiful goals.

Messi vs Neymar: The Master and The Pupil

(Barcelona 4–0 Santos, FIFA Club World Cup Final, 18 December 2011)

Although Messi is yet to win a World Cup with Argentina, he has won the FIFA Club World Cup three times with Barcelona. The second victory came in Japan in 2011, when he had the chance to play against the rising Brazilian star, and future teammate, Neymar (or Neymar da Silva Santos Júnior, to give him his full name). Neymar was only nineteen at the time, but like the young Messi, his incredible footballing talent and potential had already brought him a lot of attention. Admirers included the Brazilian footballing legend Pelé, also regarded as one of the greatest players of all time.

The match was set up by the media as a showdown between Messi and Neymar. Although Lionel was only twenty-four years old, he was already recognised as the greatest player on the planet. And on this December evening, he and his world-beating team would deliver a footballing lesson to the young, gifted Brazilian pupil.

Barcelona were favourites to win the game, and they did play incredibly well. They ended up having possession of the ball for an impressive seventy-one per cent of the game. Afterwards, their manager, Pep Guardiola, said, "In the first half, the players were like artists. Whatever they envisioned in their minds, it appeared on the pitch." But Pep and the football commentators still had to admit that Messi had stood out as the greatest artist of all.

He scored the first goal and the last. His opener, in the seventeenth minute, came at the end of a beautiful passing move. He received a through-ball inside the box on the right, and delicately chipped the ball above the approaching keeper and into the net. Santos were caught on the break for the last goal in the eighty-second minute. Again, Messi received a pass coming into the eighteen-yard box, and he danced around the keeper with perfect timing to place the ball into an empty net.

Messi was awarded the Golden Ball (usually referred to as Ballon d'Or), which is presented to the best player at the FIFA Club World Cup tournament, while Neymar received the Bronze Ball as the third most outstanding player.

However, Neymar himself had to admit that Messi and Barcelona were deserving winners. "It's impossible to stop them. Today, the best team in the world showed us how to play football."

Four years later, in 2015, Neymar would find himself back in Japan again. This time he was receiving a winner's medal in the same tournament, alongside his friend and teammate Lionel Messi.

Messi becomes the first player to score five goals in a Champions League game

(Barcelona 7–1 Bayer Leverkusen, Champions League, knockout stage, 7 March 2012)

Football is a team sport – perhaps the greatest team sport on the planet. However, once in a while, a player comes along who has the magical ability to control a game completely. To defeat the opposition single-handedly. To show his teammates, his opponents, his spectators, that one special player can make a great team a legendary one.

Barcelona walked out at their home ground Camp Nou to face Bayer Leverkusen, looking for a victory in this home leg to take them through to the last eight. Leverkusen had been runners up in the very competitive German Bundesliga the previous season, and were trailing 3–1 from the previous leg, so Barcelona were expecting their opponents to attack from the beginning. Messi came to the game on very impressive form, having already scored forty-eight goals in forty-eight games for club and country that season. At this point,

Messi was generally recognised as the best player on the planet, and Barcelona the best team. Yet despite their awareness of the enormous challenge that faced them, and their careful preparation for the game, Leverkusen could not find a way to stop Lionel the mighty flea on this occasion.

Messi's first goal broke the deadlock in the twenty-fifth minute. It came at the end of a lightning counter-attack by Barcelona. Xavi chipped a beautiful long pass into Messi's path, beyond the two central defenders. Messi ran into the box, bearing down on the keeper, then at just the right moment played a cheeky, perfectly weighted left-foot lob. Messi doubled the lead a few minutes before half-time, picking the ball up on the right-hand side of the eighteen-yard box, dancing between the defenders before striking a crisp shot into the bottom left corner of the goal.

His third goal came early in the second half, this one another delicate lob over the keeper, but this time with his right foot. The fourth goal was a fairly simple tap-in from a narrow angle, after the keeper failed to hold onto a deflected through-ball. His fifth and last goal was a much classier effort. After a series of short passes just outside the penalty area, the ball was played across to Messi's feet. After a couple of quick touches, he completed his tally with a smart, curling left-foot shot from twenty yards.

Many football commentators hailed this as perfection, a 10/10 performance from Messi. To score five goals in any professional game is no mean feat. To do it at the highest level, in the Champions League, was extraordinary. Even the disappointed Bayer Leverkusen boss Robin Dutt could only marvel at what he had witnessed that night: "Without Messi, Barca are the best team, and with him, they are in another galaxy."

Messi becomes the top goalscorer in La Liga history

(Barcelona 5–1 Sevilla, La Liga, 22 November 2014)

This was to be a historic day for Messi and for Spanish football. As Lionel arrived at the Camp Nou stadium with his friend and teammate Sergio Busquets, he was aware that he was in touching distance of Telmo Zarra's long-standing record as the top goalscorer in the history of La Liga. Despite his humble and disciplined approach to all football matches, there was a part of his mind that would keep reminding him. It was bound to happen soon, but would today be the day?

He only had to wait twenty-one minutes before he was given the opportunity to equal Zarra's goal tally. Barcelona were awarded a free kick, left of centre just outside the eighteen-yard box. Messi had already scored so many goals from a similar position in the past, but this one would mean so much more. With the ball waiting a couple of metres ahead of him, the crowd were murmuring in anticipation. Lionel glanced intensely from ball to goal, sizing up his target. With one more quick look back at the ball, he took a short run-up and struck with his legendary lethal left foot. The spinning ball whizzed just above the heads of the helpless Sevilla defenders and curled beyond the outstretched hand of the goalkeeper, right into the very top corner. Another perfect free kick to add to the collection, and now only one goal away from breaking that record.

With twenty minutes left in the second half,

Barcelona found themselves leading Sevilla 3–1, thanks to goals from Neymar and Ivan Rakitić. However, Messi's record-breaking goal still eluded him. Suddenly, in the seventy-second minute, with Sevilla pushing players forward in a desperate attempt to recover the game, Barcelona won the ball back and burst forward on the break. Messi, waiting at the halfway line, received a pinpoint pass through the middle and sprinted goalward. As the two central defenders closed in on him, he played a perfectly timed diagonal pass between them to Neymar, arriving into the eighteen-yard box on the left. Neymar took a couple of touches and was bearing down on the goal. He was in the perfect position to take a shot, and on another day, perhaps he would have done. However, from the corner of his eye he could see his Argentinian friend and teammate nearby, scampering towards the centre of the goal. Without hesitation, and without breaking his stride, Neymar slipped a perfectly weighted pass across the goal mouth. Messi slid in to poke the ball home at the far post with his right foot. *Goal!* Lionel Messi had made history.

As Messi's name flashed across the digital display

boards around the pitch, hailing his record-breaking goal, the whole Barcelona team gathered round and hugged him, then raised him in the air and gave him the bumps in celebration. Six minutes later, he would go on to complete a hat-trick, dribbling deftly across the face of the eighteen-yard box, playing a quick one-two with Neymar before slotting the ball into the bottom corner with that legendary left foot. The perfect end to a perfect match day.

"It's an amazing feeling to be the highest ever scorer in La Liga, a league with so many spectacular players in its history and players who have achieved so much. It's a great accomplishment for me."

Messi, Suárez and Neymar: the mighty trio discover their magic

(Barcelona 3–1 Atlético Madrid, 11 January 2015)

Although MSN (Messi, Suárez and Neymar) are recognised as one of the greatest attacking trios in footballing history, they did not play as a perfect goalscoring machine from the very beginning. All relationships take time to grow and develop, and so did this one. They played for many months together, learning each other's strengths and styles, before they 'clicked'. Many experts believe that their perfect footballing formula was discovered on 11 January 2015, when Barcelona took on the then La Liga champions, Atlético Madrid, at the Camp Nou.

There was a lot riding on this game. There were rumours that Messi was becoming increasingly unhappy at Barcelona. He had been left on the bench as a substitute in a recent game, and there were reports of arguments with his manager, Luis Enrique. Some Barcelona fans were worried that Lionel might be thinking about leaving and playing somewhere else in Europe. However, this game, and Messi's outstanding performance alongside his two attacking partners, would end these fears.

Messi sparkled on the night. He seemed to be everywhere, involved in every attack. In the twelfth minute of the game, he received a return pass and dribbled into the box on the right, evading defenders as he went. He directed a quick pass to Suárez, which he was able to redirect on to Neymar at the far post. Neymar slid in to score the opener.

It was Suárez's turn to score now. In the thirty-fifth minute, Messi ran onto a long pass on the right wing, just inside the opposition half. He bounced the ball off his chest and sprinted towards the penalty area, the ball glued to his feet as usual. Just as he reached the edge of the box, he laid the ball off between two defenders, into the path of Suárez. As Messi's pass and Suárez's run were timed so perfectly, the job of scoring the goal was very easy. The chemistry was working.

Although Atlético scored a very doubtful penalty in the fifty-seventh minute to keep the game alive, Messi completed the MSN goal collection a few minutes before the end of the game. A great cross-field pass from Suárez to Messi started the move. Messi controlled the high pass perfectly and tried a one-two on the edge of the box with Rakitić. The quick return pass was just too far ahead for Messi to reach. Luckily, the ball bounced off a surprised defender. Lionel was back on his feet in a flash and poked the ball into the net from the edge of the six-yard box. As he ran away from the goal, smiling ecstatically, Suárez and Neymar were with him almost immediately, hugging him and joining in with the celebrations. On that evening, it seemed clear that they were born to play together.

Lionel Messi scores his 500th Barcelona goal

(Real Madrid 2–3 Barcelona, La Liga, 23 April 2017)

This game provided another important milestone for Messi, and another chance to cross swords with his great rival, Ronaldo. Barcelona were trailing Real Madrid in La Liga, and they needed victory to stay in the race for the title.

Messi has since described it as "a perfect night, one where everything went right". This might seem a strange thing to say, given that he suffered a horrible injury in the first half. As he challenged for a low ball in midfield, an unintentional elbow from Real Madrid's Marcelo caught Messi square in the face. This blow left him lying on the floor with blood pouring from his mouth. But this game, another vital El Clásico, was too important. He needed to get back up and try to help his team to victory.

It was to be one of the most exciting and

controversial battles the two teams had ever fought. Madrid were the stronger team to start with, keeping Barcelona's goalkeeper, Marc-André ter Stegen, very busy. Eventually, Casemiro gave Real the lead with a scrambled goal.

Barcelona needed to respond quickly, and so they did five minutes later. Ivan Rakitić, holding the ball up on the right corner of a busy eighteen-yard box, spotted Messi sprinting in through the middle. The ball was played beautifully into Messi's path, but he still had a lot to do. Running at high speed, he zig-zagged between two Real defenders and slotted the ball past the keeper. 1–1.

The game continued, full of great shots, amazing saves and plenty of fouls. Both Messi and Ronaldo missed golden opportunities to put their teams ahead. But, in the seventy-third minute, it was down to Rakitić to give Barcelona the lead. He scored a wonder goal from outside the penalty area to give his team the all-important advantage.

Barcelona must have thought they were cruising to victory. In the seventy-seventh minute, Madrid's Sergio Ramos was sent off for a terrible two-footed lunge at Messi, which sent the little Argentinian rolling on the floor. But the game was far from over. James Rodríguez had just come on as a substitute. With just over five minutes left in the game, he rushed onto a low cross at the near post and clinched the equaliser.

Just as the game was heading for a score draw, Barcelona's little legend provided one last piece of magic. When he saw his teammate, Jordi Alba, receive the ball out wide, he knew this was their chance to steal the game. This was a move they had practised over and over in training. Both knew what to do without even thinking. As Messi explained later, "When Jordi gets in the final third of the field, I'll always look to drop back near the edge of the penalty area, to collect the ball and finish – and that's exactly what we did here." The ball arrived into the box, exactly when and where it was expected, and Messi's first-time shot curled beyond the keeper's desperate grasp. Messi's 500th goal for Barcelona had won the game!

Captain

Messi became captain of FC Barcelona in May 2018. Due to his quieter nature, not everyone believed he was the right choice to be captain, including Maradona (who thought he was too quiet) but the director of Barcelona says he is an example.

THE MIGHTY TRIDENT

Messi has always spoken highly of his teammates, saying that they make him a better player.

A powerful attacking trio is one of the deadliest weapons in modern football. This is often referred to as a 'trident' (a trident is a hunting weapon, a three-pronged spear that dates back to ancient history). The rise of 4-3-3 formation, following Pep Guardiola's 2008 Barcelona revolution, led to the trident strategy becoming increasingly popular, rather than the traditional use of two strikers.

Several European clubs have used the trident formation very successfully in the twenty-first century. This includes the current Liverpool team, whose front three of Mohamed Salah, Roberto Firmino and Sadio Mané are one of the most feared attacking forces in football right now.

However, possibly the most successful and potent trident in the history of the game played for Barcelona from 2014 to 2017: Messi, Suárez and Neymar, or MSN for short. In those few years together they won many trophies, including the Champions League, two La Liga titles, and three Copa del Rey finals.

Between 2014 and 2017, Messi, Neymar and Luis Suárez became known as MSN because of their goalscoring and teamwork together with assists (when you set up the ball for another player to score). They made history until Neymar left Barcelona.

Apart from being incredibly talented players individually, they were able to harmonise perfectly together on the pitch. Suárez had arrived from Liverpool FC, where he had already proved himself as a world-class goalscorer. Apart from his ability to find the net, he displayed incredible stamina and energy. Neymar left his Brazilian club, Santos, to join Messi at Barcelona in 2013. His lightning pace and magical dribbling skills often left defenders chasing shadows.

In this legendary trio, Messi was the 'conductor'. His outstanding footballing mind and instincts allowed him to be the creative playmaker. But he was also able to demonstrate the same footballing superpowers displayed by his two teammates. He was an extraordinary dribbler and a phenomenal goalscorer.

The MSN trident scored 365 goals between them in just three seasons together, before Neymar had to leave his Barcelona friends to join Paris Saint-Germain. But he would remember his partnership with these two teammates with great fondness: "The friendship that we had was something very beautiful. What I miss from Barcelona and about Barcelona is these two, due to the joy we had on a daily basis."

10

FOOTBALL LEGENDS

CLUB LOYALTIES

Throughout his entire career, Messi has only played for one team – FC Barcelona. He signed for them aged thirteen and his first appearance was when he was sixteen. He ended up in the record books (1 May 2005) as the youngest player ever who scored a goal for the franchise. He has always remained loyal, perhaps because they were the first club to invest in him; they paid for his treatment.

Messi performed regularly on the pitch and started gaining the reputation he has today; the media nicknamed him 'the Messiah' and he became a well-known favourite. Only twenty years old, he was voted the third-best player in all of Europe. Even though Messi was playing brilliantly and was an asset to the team, FC Barcelona's reputation overall was falling. They'd won the La Liga title in 2006 but each year after that they'd dropped in the rankings.

Argentina National Squad

The nickname of the Argentine national squad is La Albiceleste (meaning 'The White and Sky Blues' – the colour of their kit). Messi has sometimes had a difficult time playing at national level in both the Copa América and the World Cup.

Although Argentina as a team is one of the more successful during world cups – they won the tournament in 1978 and 1986 – a title since Messi has played for them has always been out of reach.

What Makes Messi So Special?

Being physically smaller while growing up, it was obvious that he was never going to be able to muscle his way through a team's defence – instead he learned to glide through it and became a skilful dribbler. He cuts through narrow spaces to attack defences. As previously mentioned, being shorter means he's closer to the ground. This means he can pivot quickly, which is why he's one of the world's fastest dribblers. Similar to Maradona, Messi squeezes his way through tiny spaces between defenders and other, bigger players can't get through.

The Barcelona method of play relies on many short passes – doing this requires players to have extremely good skills in this area and an ability to coordinate and create passing triangles with each other marks them out as skilful. Messi dances unpredictably around the opposition – it's much more tiring to try to catch him than a straight sprint down the wing.

OLDER, WISER, STRONGER

The later years of a great sportsperson are always tinged with a slight sense of sadness. The older they get the more questions are asked about their level of performance. "Is he past his best?" Towards the end of every great sporting career, there is an inevitable decline in the player's powers that becomes obvious to all.

The devoted fans don't want to face the harsh reality of the ageing process and its effects on their hero, and they will look for any excuse for a less-than-stellar performance. Many pundits and experts, however, hover like vultures, waiting for any failure or sign of weakness. They are ready to announce the end of an era and proclaim a new king.

So, the unavoidable question arises: has Messi's star begun to dim? The critics may well list some convincing facts and statistics. The dribbling dynamo, who has spent his career bamboozling defenders with his flickering feet, was only the fourth-most successful dribbler in 2019–20. This has been calculated based on successful dribbles per game. His old playing partner, Neymar, sits above him in the list at number two. Surprisingly, the best dribbler in the world today plays for Wolverhampton Wanderers in the Premiership – the young Spaniard Adama Traoré. He is also the fastest player, having clocked speeds close to those achieved by the world's greatest-ever sprinter, Usain Bolt!

Sponsorship

Messi has endorsements from Adidas, Pepsi, EA Sports and Turkish Airways. Adidas has sponsored Messi since 2006.

> As of 2021, Messi is one of the world's highest-paid athletes in the world, based on sponsorship deals.

The fans, on the other hand, will list the ways in which Messi has adapted his gameplay. While admitting that he has lost some of his youthful pace and dribbling prowess, they will point to improvements in his passing, shooting and overall footballing intelligence. Once he would have beaten five or six players with the ball stuck to his feet. Now he looks up, reads the situation in a split second, and plays a laser-guided through-ball straight to a striker. In many ways, they will say, he has become a more complete and more rounded player. He has matured. Less magical, but more powerful.

The critics will list his recent footballing failures. His Barcelona team came second in La Liga in the 2019–20 season, five points behind their arch-rivals, Real Madrid. They will comment that his leadership and influence on his team have weakened, and that he has started to make excuses and blame his manager and teammates for their lack of strength.

His fans will remind you that in the 2018–19 season, Messi won the European Golden Shoe for the sixth time in his career, scoring thirty-six goals in La Liga. He also won La Liga with Barcelona, scored fifty-one goals in all competitions, and was the top goalscorer in the Champions League. And in the 2019–20 season, he racked up a number of new records, including 'Most assists in a La Liga season' (twenty-one), and 'Most individual Player of the Month awards' (seven). Those fans may also argue that the reason he has shown signs of frustration is that many of his Barcelona teammates simply did not play well enough. However good he is, he can't be expected to do everything by himself.

The truth probably lies somewhere in the middle. He may not be the lightning-fast player he once was, or the very best dribbler in the world. But Lionel Messi is still an incredibly talented player with an unmatched footballing brain. As he gets older, he relies on his keen vision and finesse more than the quick feet and explosive energy of his youth. His genius now is more as a playmaker, although he still scores plenty of goals. When all his various abilities are added up, it is still hard to think of another footballer playing today that can match him. Of course, the day will come eventually when the little king will have to hand the crown to his successor. But not just yet.

Timeline

24 June 1987	Lionel Messi is born in Rosario, Argentina.
1991	Plays for Grandoli FC.
1993	Plays for Newell's Old Boys.
1997	Is diagnosed with growth hormone deficiency.
September 2000	Is invited to Spain for a trial with FC Barcelona.
21 March 2001	Officially signs with FC Barcelona.

February 2002	Finally, all the official paperwork is sorted out. Now Messi can play for his new team! Scores three goals after coming on as a sub in the second half.
16 November 2003	Debuts in a first team, aged sixteen, by playing in a friendly against Porto.
16 October 2004	Aged seventeen, makes his debut for FC Barcelona playing against Espanyol – first official match.
1 May 2005	Youngest ever goalscorer playing against Albacete – FIRST GOAL!
24 June 2005	Signs his first contract as a senior player on his eighteenth birthday.
17 August 2005	Debuts for the senior Argentina team – lasts less than sixty seconds! Is given a red card.
2007	Sets up the Leo Messi Foundation.

10 March 2007	Scores first professional hat-trick against arch-rivals Real Madrid in an El Clásico match.
27 May 2009	Header against Manchester United makes sure Barcelona won the Champions League.
2009	Is awarded Ballon d'Or for the first time.
August 2011	Is named captain of Argentina aged twenty-four.
20 March 2012	Becomes first player to score five times in a Champions League game and is now Barcelona's top goalscorer.
2 November 2012	First child, son Thiago, is born.
9 Dec 2012	Scores most goals in a calendar year.
22 Nov 2014	Scores hat-trick in Barcelona's 5–1 match against Sevilla and becomes La Liga's all-time top goalscorer.

6 June 2015	Barcelona wins Champions League final against Juventus. Barcelona have won the treble twice – the only team in history to have done this!
11 September 2015	Second child, son Mateo, is born.
30 November 2015	Is voted La Liga best player.
17 April 2016	Scores 500th goal, against Valencia.
25 November 2017	Signs new contract with Barcelona with a £626 million release clause.
30 June 2017	Marries childhood sweetheart Antonela Roccuzzo.
2018	Becomes Team Captain for Barcelona.
7 Jan 2018	His 400th appearance in La Liga equals Gerd Müller's record for most league goals.
10 March 2018	Third child, son Ciro, is born.

13 Jan 2019	Becomes first player to reach 400 goals in La Liga milestone.
23 September 2019	Wins FIFA Player of the Year.
6 November 2019	Wins sixth Ballon d'Or.
January 2020	Becomes first player in Spanish football history to win 500 matches after Barcelona beat Leganés. 500th victory in a Barca shirt – the most wins ever recorded by a single player in Spanish football.
July 2020	Barcelona's reign as La Liga champions comes to an end.

Messi's Clubs

Newell's Old Boys

Club name: Newell's Old Boys
Nickname: The Lepers (after playing in a charity match in the 1920s)
Short name: NOB
Founded: 1903, named after Isaac Newell of Kent. He was a pioneer of Argentine football.
Current manager: Gérman Burgos
Current league: Argentine Primera División
Crest: The colours of black and red were inspired by the colours of the English and German flags respectively.

Barcelona

Club name: FC Barcelona
Nickname: FCB
Short name: Barca
Founded: 1899 by Joan Gamper. He put an advert in a magazine to see if he could find anyone else interested in forming a team with him. In November of that year, he and eleven other men created the club with the name and coat of arms of Futbol Club Barcelona.
Current manager: Ronald Koeman
Current league: La Liga
Crest: The crest represents Catalonia and Spain. The two top sections have the St George's Cross and the Catalonian flag colours of red and yellow bars. In the centre of the crest are the club initials FCB. Then in the bottom section are the Barcelona team colours and a ball.

Messi's Coaches

1992 Grandoli FC

Salvador Aparicio: The story varies – some say the coach spotted him, others say it was Celia, his grandmother, who put him forward. This is what can happen with legends! "He was born knowing how to play," Aparicio has said.

1995 – 2000 Newell's Old Boys

Ernesto Vecchio coached Messi. The youth coach had spotted Messi and his talent before he even joined the old boys.

FC Barcelona

Frank Rijkaard (2003–08) gave Messi his first opportunity to play in the first team for Barcelona. Messi says he was responsible for turning him into a right-winger, even though he used to play as second striker at Newell's.

Pep Guardiola (2008–12) – Barca won the treble in 2009 with Pep as manager.

Luis Enrique (2014–17) – Barca won the treble in 2015.

Current coach: Ronald Koeman (2020–present) – In 2021, Barca went on to win six consecutive matches in La Liga under Koeman's leadership.

Speaking about Lionel's time at Barca, Koeman said, "I cannot say more about Leo ... the level he has for many years, many games…he is the most important man in the history of Barca."

Player Profile

What Position Does Messi Play?

Messi is sometimes called a 'ghost' centre forward (or striker). He floats around in any of the forward positions. He's also famous for playing the false-nine position which means deep in midfield. He drifts away from centre backs, creating uncertainty in the defence – if they stay on him, other players can easily break through but if they don't cover him, he can get through. A normal nine's role is to score.

What Skills Do You Need to Become Like Messi?

Ball control: It's not only their feet a player needs to be good at controlling the ball with, but also their head, chest and legs. Passes don't only come along the ground but in the air too and the more control you have, the better.

Dribbling: ability to move up and down the pitch, keeping the ball close to your feet. Being able to turn sharply in different directions, still with the ball close to you, sometimes at different speeds, is important.

Passing: The ability to send the ball in the direction you want it to go with accuracy is a key skill.

Spatial awareness: Knowing where you are at all times and how much space you have as well as understanding the position of each of your teammates is vital.

Tactical knowledge: knowledge of the game, how others are going to move, are vital too.

Expert Opinions

"Lionel Messi is a player who stirs feelings like no other. He turns sport into art. Every time I watch him, even on his quiet days, there are moments when you just go, 'How does he do that?' He does things three or four times in one game that I probably never managed once in my entire career. He does things no one else can … He's also quite possibly the best passer of the ball we have ever seen – he sees things that ordinary mortals don't. It's like he's watching the game from above while playing it at the same time, but even that doesn't do full justice to his genius." – Gary Lineker

"I look at the biggest players in the world and try to see what they've all got. I don't like to compare myself with people. I try to learn as much as I can from everyone around me. Definitely Messi and Ronaldo. They basically just set their lives to play football." – Raheem Sterling

"For us Argentines, Leo is as important as Maradona was. It's something that goes beyond football. He is the best in the world; playing with him in the national team is a privilege. He is generous; he shows me his movements, he teaches me to find spaces that apparently do not exist." – Lautaro Martínez

"Of those I've seen play, Messi is the best in history." – Neymar

"Messi and football are two things that go together. I enjoy watching him; he does things that nobody does. He has a stature that nobody has, something special for him, everything is special. He's a player who has football inside him, who feels it, it's incredible." – Paul Pogba

"It is clear that Messi is on a level above all others. Those who do not see that are blind." – Xavi

"Who is the best player in the world? Leo Messi. Who is the best player ever? Leo Messi." – Arsène Wenger

"I have seen the player who will inherit my place in Argentine football and his name is Messi. Messi is a genius." – Diego Maradona

"I like Messi a lot, he's a great player. Technically, we're practically at the same level." – Pelé

Records and Awards

During the 2008–09 season, Messi led Barcelona to win the Champions League, La Liga and the Copa del Rey, an accomplishment named as 'the treble'. There was no stopping Barcelona that season. They won six championships and Messi won a gold medal with Argentina at the Beijing Olympics too.

But, after the 2008 season ended, Barcelona needed to shake things up and made the decision to let the coach, Frank Rijkaard, and their star player, Ronaldinho, go.

Messi signed a new contract with the highest salary and became their main player. At one point Inter Milan expressed an interest in buying him but he wanted to stay put at Barca.

Messi discovered new ways to trick his way past defenders and in 2010 and 2011 led Barcelona to La

Liga and Spanish Super Cup championships; also in 2011, the Champions League title.

In 2012 Messi smashed records all over the place. In March, he scored five goals in a Champions League match – the first player to ever do so! A few weeks later he beat a club record set by César Rodríguez of 232 goals and became Barcelona's all-time leading scorer.

At the end of 2012, Messi had scored an amazing ninety-one goals in both club and international matches.

In January 2013, Messi broke another record when he was named the FIFA Ballon d'Or winner for the fourth time. Also in 2013, unfortunately, Messi suffered some persistent hamstring injuries, but he managed to regain record-breaking form in late 2014 to become the all-time leading scorer in La Liga and Champions League matches.

In 2015, Barcelona achieved an amazing historic second treble and Messi was honoured with his fifth FIFA Ballon d'Or trophy.

In 2019, following a further La Liga title, he claimed his sixth Ballon d'Or. Ballon d'Or, also known as the Golden Ball, is an annual award presented by France Football magazine to the football player considered to have performed the best over the previous year. Messi has won it six times (2009, 2010, 2011, 2012, 2015, 2019).

Messi tied with Cristiano Ronaldo for most Ballon d'Or wins until he won his sixth on 2 December 2019. Ronaldo wasn't actually Messi's rival for the award that year – Liverpool's Virgil van Dijk was – but Messi emerged victorious after helping Barcelona to another La Liga triumph.

Cups, Competitions and Challenges

World Cups

In both the World Cups in 2006 and 2010 Argentina reached the quarter-finals but were then eliminated by Germany – they have a history with Germany! Although they reached the 2014 final (for the fifth time), and Messi was named player of the tournament, Germany beat them.

At the 2018 World Cup in Russia, Messi's fourth, no titles were won. Messi scored an early goal in a 2–1 win over Nigeria and the win advanced them to the knockout stage, but the French team slowed his performance and his two assists weren't enough to prevent a 4–3 defeat. Sadly, it was the end for Argentina.

Not winning a World Cup title with Argentina is

the only professional ambition that Messi has yet to achieve. Fingers crossed for Qatar in 2022!

Copa América

This competition is for the best teams in South America, usually held every four years. Teams from North America and Asia have been participating since the nineties.

The Copa América loss to Chile in 2016 hit Messi hard and afterwards he announced that he was going to retire from the national team. Thousands of fans begged him to change his mind and thankfully, he did.

In 2019, Messi criticized the referees after Argentina lost to Brazil 2–0 in the Copa América semi-finals. He was given a three-game ban by the South American Football Confederation. It's only the second time in his career that he has been sent off.

League and Cup Competitions

Most countries have two footballing competitions each year. One is a league and one is a cup tournament.

La Liga is the top men's professional football division of the Spanish football league system. This competition lasts all season and is based on points – highest scorers win. To date, Messi has won ten La Liga titles with Barcelona.

Copa del Rey is an elimination tournament and with Messi playing for them, Barcelona has won seven of these titles.

Messi has won FIFA's Player of the Year six times.

The European Golden Shoe (also known as the European Golden Boot) is an award presented each season to the most prolific goalscorer in league matches from the top division of every European national league. Messi has won this six times, two times more than his rival Ronaldo.

The UEFA Champions League (sometimes known as the European Cup) is an annual competition organised by UEFA (Union of European Football Associations) where the top league teams in Europe compete. Messi playing for Barcelona has won four times.

Argentina has also won the top continental tournament, the Copa América (South American Cup).

In 2012 Messi scored ninety-one goals in sixty-nine matches, breaking Gerd Müller's record for the most goals in a single calendar year.

Messi has now scored over 672 goals for Barcelona! He is one of only seven players in his career to reach this massive milestone.

Life Beyond Football

Messi's Family

On 30 June 2017, in Rosario, Messi married Antonela Roccuzzo, his long-time girlfriend (he's known her since he was five). She's the cousin of his best friend, Lucas Scaglia, who also plays professional football.

Lionel and Antonela have three sons: Thiago, born in November 2012, Mateo, born in September 2015 and Ciro, born in March 2018. Their wedding had 260 guests and was held at a luxury hotel in Rosario, with a number of fellow star footballers.

Tattoos

Messi is recognised by his many colourful tattoos. One of the first tattoos Messi got was the face of his mother, Celia, which is situated on his left shoulder blade. He has a very close relationship with his mother. The images on Messi's left leg are of Thiago's hands along with his name on his calf. He also has the number 10 – which he wears for both club and country – and a football on his shin. In 2018, just above the ankle on his right leg, Messi now has the names and birth dates of all three of his sons: Thiago, Mateo and Ciro. There's a large area of black on that leg where he had old designs covered over.

On his right arm, tattoos create a 'sleeve'. At the top is an image of Jesus Christ in a crown of thorns, most likely inspired by his religious beliefs. An eye adorns the inside of his bicep and a small crown. His tattooist Roberto Lopez has said about the artwork: "The lotus symbolises that talent can grow anywhere even with forces stopping it. The rose window of the famous Barcelona church Sagrada Familia shows the love he has for the city." That's on his elbow, while a budding red rose, a pink lotus and orange flowers are on the arm too.

An old-fashioned pocket watch is on Messi's forearm.

Messi also has a tattoo dedicated to his wife Antonela on his left hip: a pair of red lips.

Charity and UNICEF

Messi is well known for being quiet and unshowy off the pitch, but he likes to quietly help others, perhaps because of the medical difficulties he suffered himself when he was younger. In 2007 he founded the Leo Messi Foundation, a non-profit organisation created to give all children the same chances to make their dreams a reality. The foundation provides opportunities for disadvantaged youths. In February 2019, the foundation donated £170,000 to UNICEF for projects in Kenya.

Messi has contributed to UNICEF (United Nations International Children's Emergency Fund) since 2004 with both his time and money. In 2010, UNICEF named Messi a goodwill ambassador, with a focus on fighting for children's rights across the globe.

He's also given back to his old club in Rosario, Newell's Old Boys, helping them to build a gym.

More recently, in 2020 when the coronavirus

pandemic struck the world, whilst football was suspended, Barcelona players cut their wages by seventy per cent in order to help the club. It wasn't compulsory but there was an expectation that players would do this. Messi did, and in addition, he personally donated over 1 million euros to hospitals to help them buy equipment. His old coach Pep Guardiola (now coach of Man City) also donated a million.

In His Own Words

Playing Style

"My style of play has always been the same. I never tried to develop a specific style. From very young I just played this way. What is certainly true is that I learnt a lot in the youth system. The way we worked here was different. There was a lot of contact with the ball and a lot of work on the tactical system. I came from Argentina where we didn't do anything like that. Over there it was lots of running and not much more.

I'm more critical with myself than anyone else is. I know when I have done well and when I have done badly. I don't need anyone to tell me. I just look at what I did on the pitch and I know; I don't need to be told anything else.

I try to improve every day. If people compare me to players like that, players who were greats and are still talked about today after they have retired, then that's lovely. But I don't think about that. I think about improving all the time and at the end of my career I'll think about what I did. Then let people judge."

Messi on Other Players

"Xavi is a great player. He never loses the ball, he has great vision and reads the game, he controls the rhythm and pace. Andrés Iniesta is similar. Maybe Andrés has more goalscoring ability, he gets into the area more, arriving from deeper. But they're similar. Andrés has great vision too and when he is on form the team revolves round him. When he and Xavi are both on the pitch it's hard for the other team to get the ball."

"Neymar was a very happy person, he was always happy, he had fun both on and off the court. When he was in the dressing room he was always happy, and he provided a special joy. He is one of the best and contributed us a lot on the field. But it is understandable that people can think like that since he left in a way he did not like. Neymar is one of the best players in the world, and I would love for him to return."

"Lautaro is spectacular. He has impressive qualities. You could tell he was going to be a great player and he is showing that. He's very strong, really good one on one, scores a lot of goals and in the area he fights with anyone, holds it up, he can turn, scrap to win it all on his own. He has a lot of quality. He's very complete."

The Future

"My idea is to stay at Barca, and as long as the club and the fans want that, there is no problem on my behalf. I want to win another Champions League with Barca, and I also want to continue winning La Liga titles here. My idea is to stay at the club and try to aspire to every honour again. At no time has leaving Barca crossed my mind, and it hasn't now either. The years go by and you never know, but I feel very good. I feel better overall than in previous seasons. The club don't do whatever I want. I don't make the decisions at Barca."